IMAGINE THAT™

Licensed exclusively to Imagine That Publishing Ltd
Tide Mill Way, Woodbridge, Suffolk, IP12 1AP, UK
www.imaginethat.com
Copyright © 2020 Imagine That Group Ltd
All rights reserved
4 6 8 9 7 5
Manufactured in China

Written by Jamie French
Illustrated by Lucy Barnard

ISBN 978-1-78958-307-6

A catalogue record for this book is available from the British Library

THE
NUTCRACKER

Written by Jamie French
Illustrated by Lucy Barnard

It was Christmas Eve and there was going to be a big party. The Christmas tree sparkled with lights and baubles.

'It's so pretty!' cried Marie.

Soon, the guests arrived.
The house was filled with
music and dancing.

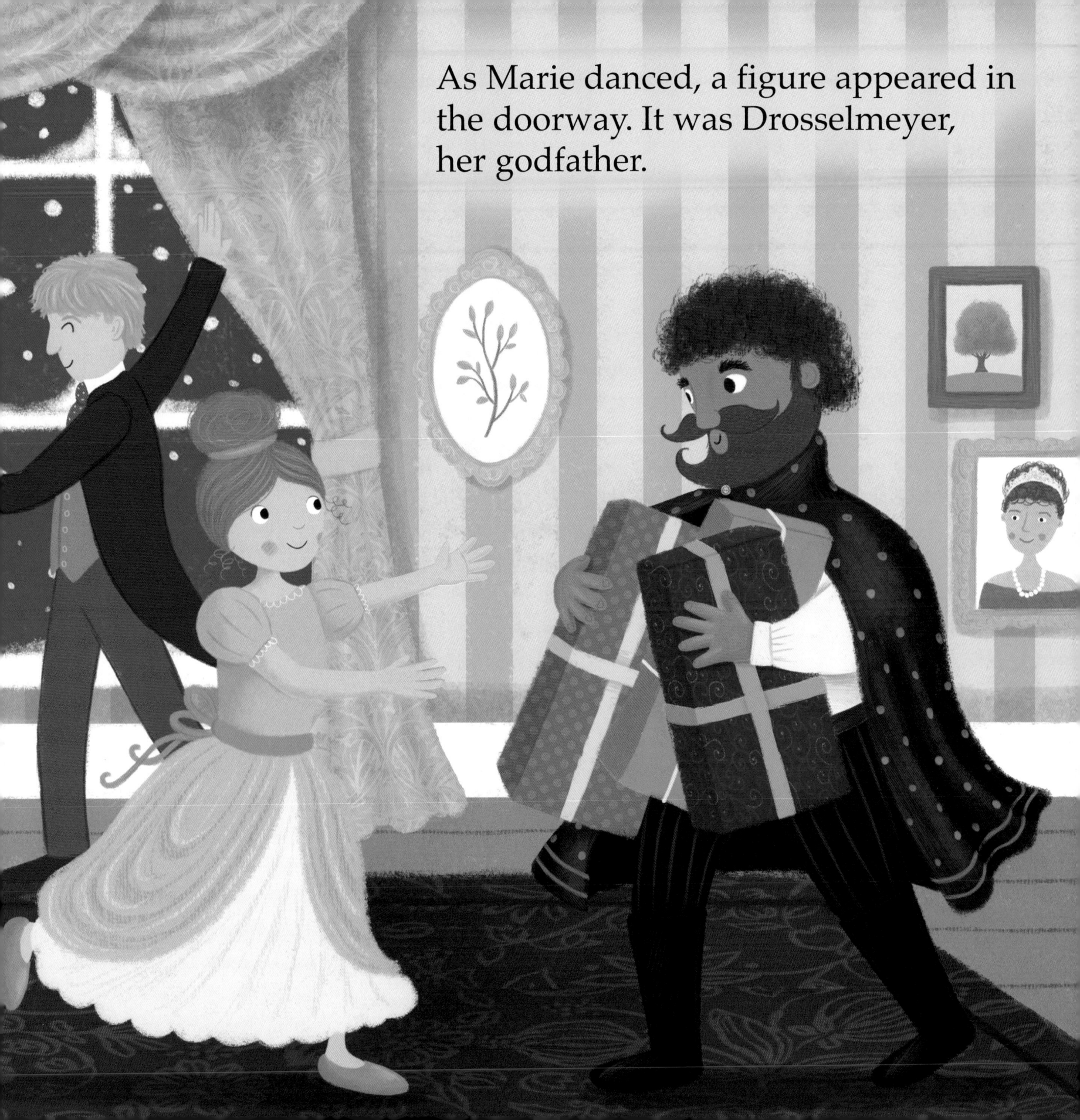

As Marie danced, a figure appeared in the doorway. It was Drosselmeyer, her godfather.

Drosselmeyer was a famous toymaker –
and he had brought gifts for everyone.

Drosselmeyer had an extra special gift for Marie. It was a wooden Nutcracker in the shape of a man.

Marie loved playing with her Nutcracker,
but her brother was jealous. 'It's not fair!'
he cried.

Then he grabbed the Nutcracker and threw it across the room. *Crack!* went its head as it hit the floor.

Marie ran to pick up her Nutcracker,
tears rolling down her cheeks.

Very carefully, she wrapped a ribbon
around the Nutcracker's broken head.
Then she placed him under the
Christmas tree and went to bed.

Marie couldn't sleep so she crept downstairs
to give her Nutcracker a hug.

As the clock struck twelve, something magical
happened. Huge mice appeared from the corners
of the room. And the Christmas tree started to grow!

The Nutcracker started to grow too –
and big toy soldiers appeared.
Bravely, the Nutcracker and the toy
soldiers battled the fearsome mice.

'Look out!' called Marie, as the Mouse King attacked the Nutcracker. She threw her slipper at the mouse and he fell down.

The mice disappeared, beaten.

Suddenly, glittery snowflakes flurried around Marie,
and in the Nutcracker's place stood a handsome Prince.

'You have saved me,' he said. 'Come with me to my kingdom – the *Land of Sweets*.'

Marie and the Prince were greeted by the pretty Sugar Plum Fairy. The Prince explained how Marie had saved his life.

To celebrate, the Sugar Plum Fairy put on a dance show. Everyone was dressed as sweets.

Soon it was time for the last dance.

As the Sugar Plum Fairy and her sweetheart danced for Marie and the Prince, a magical sleigh appeared to take them home.

'Remember me,' whispered the Prince as they flew away.

Ding-dong-ding! went the Christmas Day bells. Marie awoke from the strangest dream and ran to pick up the Nutcracker. 'I love you so much,' she said.

And with that, the Nutcracker disappeared. In his place stood the Prince from Marie's night-time adventure!

'Your love has freed me from an evil spell!' laughed the Prince, spinning Marie around and around.

Years later, Marie and her Prince got married – and went to live happily ever after in the *Land of Sweets*.